The Cow Said BOO!

by Lana Button

Illustrations by Alice Carter

pajamapress

One day the cow had such a cold
that when she tried to **"MOO,"**
her nose was super stuffy
and the cow said,

That cold had made her miserable

(and kind of clumsy, too).

She crashed into the clothesline and…

She greeted all the animals
(as cows politely do).

She tried to moo, "good morning."
But the cow said, **"BOO!"**

"Awk!" the rooster crowed.
"What do we cock-a-doodle do?"

They thought
the farm was *haunted*
when the cow said, **"BOO!"**

They couldn't recognize their friend,
So what's a cow to do?

She tried to moo, "goodbye, then."

But the cow said, "**Boooo**."

But…

That night she spied
a fearsome fox

And then she bravely knew:
She had to save her friends. And so…

The friends let out a cheer:
"Our cow's a hero through and through!"
But she did 3 big sneezes, then...

…the cow said,

"BOO!"

They nursed her back to health until the cow could **"Mooo"** away!

She wasn't one bit stuffy. But—

First published in Canada and the United States in 2021

Text copyright © 2021 Lana button

Illustration copyright © 2021 Alice Carter

This edition copyright © 2021 Pajama Press Inc.

This is a first edition.

10 9 8 7 6 5 4 3 2 1

Canada Council for the Arts   Conseil des arts du Canada

ONTARIO ARTS COUNCIL
CONSEIL DES ARTS DE L'ONTARIO
an Ontario government agency
un organisme du gouvernement de l'Ontario

Canada

The publisher gratefully acknowledges the support of the Canada Council for the Arts and the Ontario Arts Council for its publishing program. We acknowledge the financial support of the Government of Canada through the Canada Book Fund (CBF) for our publishing activities.

Library and Archives Canada Cataloguing in Publication
Title: The cow said "boo!" / by Lana Button ; illustrations by Alice Carter.
Names: Button, Lana, 1968- author. | Carter, Alice, illustrator.
Description: First edition.
Identifiers: Canadiana 20210153717 | ISBN 9781772782165 (hardcover)
Subjects: LCGFT: Stories in rhyme.
Classification: LCC PS8603.U87 C69 2021 | DDC jC813/.6—dc23

Publisher Cataloging-in-Publication Data (U.S.)
Names: Button, Lana, 1968-, author. | Carter, Alice, illustrator.
Title: The Cow Said "BOO!" / by Lana Button ; illustrations by Alice Carter.
Description: Toronto, Ontario Canada : Pajama Press, 2021. | Summary: "In rhyming quatrains with a chant-along refrain, a sick cow has a run-in with a sheet on a clothesline and is mistaken for a ghost because her stuffed-up nose turns every "moo" to "boo." She is disheartened when her friends are frightened of her, but she uses the situation to her advantage to scare off a marauding fox. Recognized at last, the cow is nursed back to health by her friends, but a lighthearted twist suggests that the cold is contagious"— Provided by publisher.
Identifiers: ISBN 978-1-77278-216-5 (hardcover)
Subjects: LCSH: Ghosts – Juvenile fiction. | Domestic animals —Juvenile fiction. | Humorous fiction. | Stories in rhyme. | BISAC: JUVE-NILE FICTION / Animals / Farm Animals. | JUVENILE FICTION / Holidays & Celebrations / Halloween. | JUVENILE FICTION / Health & Daily Living / Diseases, Illnesses & Injuries.
Classification: LCC PZ7.B888Co | DDC [E] – dc23

Original art created with colored pencil, watercolor, and digital media
Cover and book design— Lorena González Guillén

Manufactured in China by WKT Company

Pajama Press Inc.
469 Richmond St. E, Toronto, ON M5A 1R1

Distributed in Canada by UTP Distribution
5201 Dufferin Street Toronto, Ontario Canada, M3H 5T8

Distributed in the U.S. by Ingram Publisher Services
1 Ingram Blvd. La Vergne, TN 37086, USA

To my dad,
for cheering me along all the way!
—L.B.

For Nick and Shannon,
and all the animals they love!
—A.C.

Scare away colds.
Wash your hooves and paws!

1. Water

2. Soap